# YOUNG CLAUS
## *Legend Of the Boy Who Became Santa*

*An Original Story by*
## J. Michael Sims

**Cygnet Trumpeter**
*Publishers*

# YOUNG CLAUS
*Legend of the Boy Who Became Santa*

Copyright © 1996 by YC, Ltd. Co.

Austin, Texas

CYGNET TRUMPETER
Publishers
A SWANALLIANCE Entertainment Company
P.O. Box 491626
Los Angeles, California 90049-8626

This book is printed on acid-free, recycled paper.

## Publisher's Cataloging in Publication

Sims, J. Michael.
    Young Claus : legend of the boy who became Santa / an original story by J. Michael Sims.
    p. cm.
    Preassigned LCCN: 95-68713.
    ISBN 0-9645976-6-7

    1. Santa Claus–Fiction. 2. Christmas–Fiction. I. Title.
PZ7.S567You 1995             [Fic]
                           QBI95-20487

Summary: Orphaned as a small child, Young Claus sets off to find his destiny and enters a fantasia filled forest inhabited by a giant, an evil bruin, mystic elves and talking animals. This rebellious young man eventually learns the gift of sharing, love, and self-purpose in life and returns to his orphanage, and to this world, to spread good cheer and happiness to children everywhere.

First in a series of YOUNG CLAUS books

Printed in the United States of America

# AUTHOR'S NOTE

When my children were young, I wrote this story about the joy of giving, to be read aloud one chapter each night, ending on Christmas Eve.

I urge you to share it in the same way, over several nights. The ten to fifteen minutes a night you spend reading YOUNG CLAUS to your children will be the greatest Christmas gift they—or you—will ever receive, not because of the story, but because your presence is so much more important than your presents.

*J. Michael Sims*

*To Christopher, Jonathan, Elizabeth, their mother Catherine, and all the young friends and wonderful ideas they have brought into my life.*

THE LEGEND BEGINS...

# CHAPTER ONE

It all began long, long ago, on a cold, clear mid-winter's eve, a fortnight before Christmas. Nine ragged orphans were struggling up a steep, snow covered slope. Young Claus, as usual, was bringing up the rear, pulling the only thing he could really call his own—the red, handmade sled that brought him to the gates of the orphanage as a stout, blond-haired baby. Young Claus had lived at the Mother of Mercy Home for over ten years. No one knew how old he was or where he had come from.

Basically, Claus was a happy boy, full of mischief and fun. He had a special way about him—he could make children laugh even when there seemed to be nothing to laugh about. But he had a serious side too. Since he had not known where he had come from, he thought it was very important to know where he was going in life. And, so far, he didn't have a clue.

On this particular day, Claus wasn't thinking about his future and the children weren't smiling. They had worked hard all day gathering winter nuts and berries and were very tired as they trudged up the snowy slope.

The food they had collected filled two rough-sewn bags tied onto Claus' sled. This ragged work-party was led by twelve-year-old Elder Anna, who held firmly to the tiny hand of Baby Anna. Baby Anna was "four and three months" as she liked to put it. Elder Anna had been just plain Anna until Baby Anna was brought to Mother of Mercy the year before, her name stitched neatly into her coarse, homespun blouse. Rather than change either girl's name, the nuns called them Elder Anna and Baby Anna. Her name, after all, was the only thing the sad little girl brought to Mother of Mercy. Baby Anna, when the kind woodcutter found her, wouldn't speak to anyone —until she met the Elder Anna.

Of course, as a baby, she couldn't speak very clearly, even to Elder Anna. She could only say the letter "N," for example, when it was in the middle of a word—like "Anna." That's how Young Claus became "Claus." When Baby Anna tried to say his real name—Nicholas— all she could say was "An-na-koss." Young Nicholas thought being called "Anna Claus" was funny, at first, but when the other kids named him "Anna-3," he asked Baby Anna to just call him "Claus." Since she could say "Kaloss," she was very happy, and Nicholas soon became "Claus," just as Anna had become Elder Anna to all the other orphans.

Elder Anna, like Young Claus, had a special way with children. They obeyed her as they would an adult, because she thought like an adult, but loved her as they would another child, because she always treated them with respect. The nuns at the orphanage were nice and caring, but naturally treated the children as children instead of people.

Soon after the Annas met, Baby Anna stuck to Elder Anna like a shadow. That is why the little girl was in the work group. Elder Anna loved and accepted Baby Anna as a sister. And she accepted the responsibility for her as she accepted all responsibility—with a quiet smile.

Elder Anna knew the long climb through the deep snow had tired the children so she called out encouragement without looking back, "Come, children, we're almost over this one! Keep going!"

And everyone did. Everyone except Young Claus, that is. Claus had stopped to stare back down the snow-blanketed hillside. Since they had climbed the steep slope at an angle, the snow below him stretched bright and unbroken for two hundred yards or more. Claus glanced at his heavy-laden sled, then back at the inviting slope. He thought of the day's hard work, then of the evening's long journey. It was more than he could stand.

With a joyful whoop that startled the others, he whipped his sled around, leaped atop the bags, and was off like a shot. Claus picked up speed quickly and the other children began to laugh and clap and slide after him down the slope. Baby Anna broke away to share in the moment of carefree fun.

Elder Anna, standing almost on the crest of the hill, watched with a sad smile, happy that her charges still had the gift of laughter despite their hard lives. Then suddenly, Elder Anna's face changed. She looked up the mountain. There was something in the air. Elder Anna spoke loudly, with authority. "Children…"

They all turned to look at her, smiles still on their faces. As Elder Anna opened her mouth to speak again, Claus hit a huge bump that sent him, his sled, and the contents of the larder-bags bouncing hurry-scurry down the last forty yards of the slope. Elder Anna burst into laughter at the sight of the boy sprawling down the hill. The others turned in time to see Claus pile into a deep snowdrift at the foot of a huge evergreen. Crash! Their laughter was loud and happy but died quickly when Claus did not climb from the drift.

Elder Anna broke the sudden silence as she screamed Claus' name and started sliding down the slope as fast as she could. Suddenly, Claus sat up grinning, then laughing, very pleased with his little joke. Elder Anna was not amused, though the other orphans were. She stopped and called out in anger to the mischievous boy.

"Young Claus," (she always added the "young" when Claus did something foolish), "Young Claus, you have cost us all precious time and strength. You will answer for it."

With that, Elder Anna whirled and started back up the hill. The children followed, still chuckling.

Claus grinned at Elder Anna's warning, grabbed his heart, and collapsed back in the snowdrift in a pretend faint. After a moment, he chuckled and sat up to see Elder Anna, with Baby Anna in her arms, standing on the hilltop, looking down at him.

Elder Anna shouted at the boy far below, "The Pole Wind blows a storm off the mountain, Young Claus. Do not delay."

Claus jumped to his feet and started grabbing scattered nuts and berries in a fit of pretend terror.

Elder Anna frowned at the boy's actions, then turned to the others. "We must hurry, children, or the night and the storm will be upon us."

Claus, ignoring Elder Anna's wise warning, began to play in the snow, jumping into deep drifts, throwing himself into the snow in different shapes, pulling his sled partway up the hillside to slide down again. Finally exhausted, Claus fell on his back and began to make "Angel Wings" in the snow. The hillside and valley were silent and Claus closed his eyes and smiled, all alone and very happy.

# CHAPTER TWO

The frozen silence was broken by scuffling and snuffling noises from somewhere nearby. Claus opened his eyes, sat up slowly, and listened. He figured out the direction the sound was coming from, then slowly stood to move into the trees toward it. A few yards into the forest, he spied the source of the sound—a scrawny, ancient moose was on its hind legs, trying with all its might to snatch the last bit of leaf from an icy oak tree.

Claus kneeled and shaped a snowball, then sneaked slowly, carefully, quietly, toward the hungry moose. As soon as the boy was close enough, he let fly and, with a perfect shot, hit the poor moose on the rump. The startled moose, terrified, scampered away as fast as his weak legs would carry him. Claus, not satisfied, chased the poor creature into the forest before finally giving up with a laugh. It was not an evil laugh. In all fairness, Claus simply did not realize that the old moose was starving.

The other children were slipping and sliding down the next-to-last hill before their village.

Elder Anna called out encouragement. "One more hill, children, just one more, and then we'll be home."

She looked back up to their tracks in the snow and thought about Claus. Her fear of the storm was growing, but she would not worry the others.

Claus, meanwhile, had retrieved his sled and the larder bags and was picking up the nuts and berries that lay scattered across the hillside. Suddenly he stopped, threw his arms up and fell back in the snow with a whoop. Then he began, again, to make Angel Wings. Claus lay there for a long time, slowly moving his arms up and down. Finally, he drew in a lungful of cold air, smiled, and stopped his wings.

After a moment, he sighed and opened his eyes. Suddenly, Claus felt fear as he noticed that the sky above him had changed. Where bright sunlight once glared off the snow, there was only gray. And it was growing darker by the moment.

Claus sat up. The pole wind was bringing darkness down the mountain like a great blanket. Claus clambered to his feet and began frantically grabbing handful of nuts and berries, jamming them into the limp larder bags.

Elder Anna, carrying Baby Anna, topped the last hill and stopped. The other children struggled after her. When they had all gathered on the hilltop she put Baby Anna into another child's arms.

"I must go back for Claus," she announced quietly.

Baby Anna began to cry, but the other children pressed on toward the warmth of the orphanage.

Claus was racing up and down the hillside when the storm's first snow blew in. He grabbed for a nut, but the Pole Wind blew it from his reach. The blast of icy wind almost knocked Claus into the snow. At first, Claus tried to catch the nuts and berries as the storm scattered them up the hill. He soon gave up—his foolishness had cost them the day's food gathering.

He turned with his empty sled to follow his friends' tracks up the hillside. The new snow soon turned Claus' eyebrows frosty white, but he was pleased about one thing—the terrible Pole Wind would be at his back. Elder Anna, already climbing another hill, knew the storm had hit Claus, just as she knew earlier that it was coming. She moved faster, praying silently for her friend.

The Pole Wind's fury grew stronger as Claus tried to follow the rapidly disappearing tracks of the other orphans. Then he stumbled, sliding back down the slope. He had recovered and taken a few more steps when the first whiteout hit and blasted away his already numbed sense of direction. Claus felt like someone had wrapped his head in frozen blinders—he could see nothing but pure white as the wind knocked him still further down the icy slope.

Elder Anna saw the storm coming and braced herself for the blast. She cried out for Claus but her shout was lost as the growing storm hit her full-force.

Claus was confused by the fierce whiteout as he climbed the steep hill for the third time. He had forgotten that the Pole Wind should be at his back. Now, he was heading in the wrong direction, into the mountains and away from Elder Anna and the orphanage. Elder Anna was making progress against the terrible storm until the whiteout swallowed her. She dropped to her knees too late—the wind slammed her into the snow and swept her back down the hill she had been climbing. She rolled into a ball when she stopped sliding and lay still, hoping for the blinding storm to pass quickly.

Claus came to the top of his slope at last and fell to his back so he could rest. The snowfall grew heavier so he climbed to his feet, fell on the sled, and shot down the opposite slope. Snow stung his face as he sped down the steep hillside. Sled and boy finally bumped to a halt and Claus started toward the next hill, which he could barely see. The storm lashed at his face as he moved deeper into the freezing mountains.

Elder Anna was only two hills away from

Claus, shouting his name at the top of her voice. Claus was climbing another hill, still facing the storm when he thought he heard something. No, he reasoned, "I didn't hear anything" and trudged on. He thought Elder Anna was already back at the orphanage warming her feet in front of the fire. He was nearing the top of a three-sided hill, hoping for a better view, when he heard his name. He stopped and shouted back.

Elder Anna brightened and shouted again. Yes, Claus had answered!

Claus was relieved and said a prayer of thanks as he neared the top of his storm-blasted look-out post.

Elder Anna, smiling while she fought the wind, also said a silent prayer of thank you.

Claus was so tired he had to climb the last few yards of the hill on his hands and knees. It was difficult and painful, but he knew he would soon be safe. At last, he pulled himself over the crest of the hill only to look into the angry face of a monstrous bear. The huge bruin's eyes glowed black with evil and his teeth glinted yellow with hunger.

With a mighty roar, the bear charged Young Claus. The boy stumbled away, terrified, and fell on his sled.

Elder Anna heard the roar and broke into a struggling, snow-bound run.

Claus and his sled were flying down the northern slope, totally out of control. The bear was roaring after him when the sled hit a bump and went tumbling down the steep slope. Claus held onto the sled's rope with all his might. Then the second whiteout hit and, suddenly, Claus was speeding down a slope he could not see.

Elder Anna curled up, praying, and waited for the whiteout to pass. The bear, too, curled up to wait. By the time a new blast from the Pole sent the whiteout down the mountain, Claus was far away from the bear—and from Elder Anna. He called her name, but not too loudly for fear of the evil bruin. He didn't need to worry—the storm swallowed his voice. The bear, confused and furious, shuffled on into the mountains in roughly the same direction as Claus.

Elder Anna, true to her giving nature, looked for Young Claus until she could look no more.

Claus, cold and frightened, climbed hill after hill in the fearful storm. Finally, he knew he was lost and soon began to lose hope. The wind and snow and ice blasted away his strength until he collapsed on the side of a snow-covered slope deep in the mountains. There, Young Claus curled up, braced his only possession against the wind, and closed his eyes. At first, the snow only drifted up against the sled, but soon it began to cover both sled and boy. Claus huddled closer under the sled and curled up. The boy and the sled disappeared under the blowing snow to become little more than another snowy mound on the side of the icy mountain.

# CHAPTER THREE

On the hillside where Claus lay buried in the snow and ice, the storm had passed. The winter night was clear and bright with stars—and very, very still.

At the orphanage, the other children prayed silently. At that moment, one star shined brighter than all the others, and, for a second, its light gleamed off the snow-covered mound that was Young Claus.

Suddenly, in the distance a wolf howled, then another and another and another until the hillside echoed with their beastly baying. The pack had caught the scent of Young Claus and its howls grew louder and louder and more and more ferocious as they fought each other to be the first to reach the boy.

Still, Claus did not move. The wolves arrived—growling, fighting, snapping, biting at each other as they began to dig and claw at the icy snow that protected the sleeping boy. Just as the ravenous wolves broke through the crust of Claus' frozen blanket, a giant, gentle voice echoed across the hillside.

"Thank you, Sobaka."

There was a powerful growl and the wolves stopped their digging. Most of the pack moved away, but three of the most ferocious beasts started scratching and clawing again. That commanding growl finally sent the trio sulking after the others.

Against the bright night sky, two figures were silhouetted, one on four legs, the other on two. Sobaka, the Wisest of Wolves, growled gently at the giant figure beside him, then padded calmly after his pack.

The huge man knelt in the snow to dig Young Claus out. The boy's fingers were frozen to the sled rope and could not be pried loose. The giant finally stopped trying to separate his fingers and lifted Claus and the sled gently into his arms. The only sound was the giant's snowshoes crackling across the snow as he moved slowly down the hillside, Claus' sled bouncing against his knees.

———————

Claus was sleeping on the hearth of a giant fireplace, his face toward the crackling fire. His precious sled, finally free from his grasp, leaned against the hearth nearby. On the mantle, far above Claus, sat a hand-carved manger scene; it was, after all, only a short time before Christmas. The massive fireplace made Young Claus look even smaller. He was being watched by a squirrel with a bandaged tail and two timid rabbits when, suddenly, a raccoon clambered atop the boy. The raccoon, his eyes alert to any danger, pulled at Claus' clothes and blonde hair. Then, suddenly, Claus stirred, sending the forest animals scurrying away.

The boy opened his eyes slowly. All he could see were the enormous dancing flames in front of him. His eyes widened in fear, but he closed them quickly and began to pray. His prayer was interrupted by a huge, deep chuckle. Claus squinted his eyes tighter and prayed faster.

Another chuckle stopped him. Claus opened his eyes, puzzled, doubting that the gentle laughter he heard could be evil, even if it was so loud. He looked around slowly, carefully, and finally realized he was in front of a fireplace—a fireplace five times as large as any he had ever seen. Claus slowly rolled to his back and looked into the huge face of a kind man. Claus' rescuer spoke and his deep voice seemed to shake even the flames.

"You are better, I see."

Claus only stared.

"You must eat."

Suddenly, the man stood up. To the small boy, it seemed like he stood and stood and stood. He was a giant, almost eight feet tall. The giant spoke again, "I am called Mountain."

Claus nodded and whispered, "the name fits you well."

Mountain roared with laughter, then grabbed a bowl from his huge table. Claus sat up to watch the giant and looked around the room for the first time. It was clearly a giant's cabin. Everything was made to Mountain's size—the cabinet, the chairs, the bed, the bowls, the earthen cookware. Claus felt very small as he watched Mountain ladle broth into the huge bowl.

Suddenly, Claus remembered Elder Anna and panic filled his voice. "Elder Anna, where is Elder Anna?"

Mountain shook his mighty head slowly, "I know no one by that name."

"She was on the mountain with me," cried Claus.

Mountain, concerned, shook his head thoughtfully. Claus lay back, tears filling his eyes. Then he sat up and tried to stand. "We must look, Mountain, we must look!"

But he was too weak to stand and fell off the hearth. It was a fall of several feet and Mountain rushed to the boy's side and gently placed him back on his bed.

The giant spoke gently, "If she was near, I would know. The animals would tell me."

Claus began to cry. "She tried to help me, in the storm. She came back for me."

Mountain kneeled and put his huge hand on the boy's shoulder to comfort him. As he closed his eyes, Claus saw Elder Anna on the hilltop. She held Baby Anna in her arms. After a long time, Claus finally cried himself to sleep, sure that Elder Anna was gone forever because of his foolishness.

Claus finally woke the following day. He was still very weak but his empty stomach growled like the angry bear and drove all thoughts but food from his tired brain. Mountain was ready and served the boy bread and broth. Claus ate the giant's portion and asked for more. While Claus ate, Mountain sat across from him. The squirrel with the bandaged tail sat on the arm of Mountain's chair.

"What is your name, lad?" Mountain asked. Claus told him.

"It is a fine name," the giant replied. "And what brought you so deep into the mountains?"

Claus thought for a moment, then answered, "My sled and my foolishness."

Claus told him the whole story, then

Mountain spoke again, nodding. "You have much to learn, Young Claus, but you have taken the first step by knowing and admitting you were wrong."

Claus smiled, but Mountain's "Young Claus" made him think of Elder Anna and Baby Anna.

"What troubles you so?" Mountain asked gently.

Claus reminded the giant about Elder Anna, then added, "and now Baby Anna must feel sad again, and as lonely as she did before she came into the orphanage. "

Mountain felt very sorry for Young Claus, "The hurt will heal, young friend, the hurt will heal."

Then the gentle giant tried to get Claus' mind off the Annas.

"Today is the day," Mountain said, "when we remove the bandage from Taku's tail."

He put out a huge finger and rubbed the squirrel's head. Taku ran up the giant's arm and sat on his shoulder while Mountain stood and moved over to a small table (at least, it was "giant-sized" small) near the fireplace. The giant bent over the table and signaled for Claus to sit up on the hearth for a better view. Claus was still feeling sorry for Baby Anna—and himself—but he sat up, curiosity aroused.

Taku was nervous and scampered around the giant's hand and arm like it was a branch in a tree. Mountain chose a fine, delicate knife from several on the cloth-covered table. Taku grew very still. Mountain gently slit the bandage, then slowly rolled it off the squirrel's tail and removed the tiny splints.

Except for the hair that was missing where the bandage had been, Taku's tail was as good as new. He flicked it, as squirrels do, several times. Perfect. Taku scampered here and there, stopping only to flick and admire his mended tail. Claus' sadness soon turned to laughter as he watched the squirrel's happy antics.

But the merriment tired the boy and Mountain made him lie down again.

"You will need much rest, Young Claus, before you can safely leave my hearth," said Mountain.

Claus settled in, ready for a nap. Then his thoughts returned to the Annas...especially

Baby Anna. He saw her every time he closed his eyes. Elder Anna had breathed life and laughter back into the lonely little girl's soul. If Claus was terribly sad—and he was—then Baby Anna must be heartbroken. He asked Mountain to move the sled closer.

That night, Claus dreamed of Baby Anna; she was lying on Elder Anna's bed, crying in her sleep. Claus woke up with a start. He sat up, then moved slowly to the great cabin door and pushed it open.

On the snow-covered hill just outside Mountain's cabin, Young Claus fell to his knees and looked up into the black winter sky. The stars were crisp, the moon only a crescent. And one star twinkled brighter than all the others for a moment.

# CHAPTER FOUR

The following morning, the boy, who felt much better, and the giant walked slowly, side by side, down a snow-packed trail that led to a great frozen river at the foot of Mountain's mountain. Claus' sled was sliding backwards down the gentle slope in front of him; he held tight to the rope. Mountain's washtub-size wooden bucket sat on the sled.

"Mountain," Claus spoke without looking up, "do you believe in Heaven?"

Mountain was a bit surprised at the question. "Yes, Young Claus, I do."

"Do you think Elder Anna is in Heaven?" Claus asked.

Mountain smiled, "If she is as you have said— a kind and gentle soul—then I am sure she is."

Claus thought for a moment, "Good," he said, finally.

They walked in silence. Mountain led the way

to the water hole he kept open when the river had turned to ice. Next to the hole in the ice was a small bucket with a short rope attached. Holding onto the rope, Claus dropped the bucket into the flowing water, then spoke again.

"Mountain…"

The giant knew something was on the boy's mind. "Yes, Young Claus?"

"I must return to the orphanage as soon as possible."

Mountain studied the boy's face, "Why 'as soon as possible,' my young friend?"

Claus pulled the bucket from the hole. It was so full, he spilled most of the water before clearing the rim of ice. "Because I must take Elder Anna's place," answered Claus.

Mountain spoke gently. "You must walk your own path, Young Claus. What is done, is done."

Claus dumped water from the small bucket into the larger one on his sled. "Do you mean I should not go back?"

"No," answered Mountain, "I mean that the orphanage may not hold your destiny. But I cannot say for sure. I cannot read your Book of Life."

Claus was very thoughtful as he dropped the small bucket back down the hole for more water. Both Claus and Mountain were still deep in thought when the wolf appeared behind them. Claus saw the beast first in the reflection of the water and shouted as he swung the small bucket at the surprised wolf. Mountain whirled and immediately jumped up to grab the bucketful of water before it hit the wolf.

"No!" the giant shouted.

Claus was surprised and stared as the wolf collapsed even though the bucket didn't hit him.

"He is hurt," Mountain said as he hurried to the wolf's side.

The poor creature was not only injured but starving and almost dead. Mountain gently gathered the wolf into his arms and started for the cabin.

"Young Claus," Mountain said angrily over his shoulder, "you must learn to look inside God's creatures, beyond the fur and teeth. Fill the bucket quickly and come along. We will need the water." With that, Mountain's giant steps took him quickly up the frozen riverbank and Claus was alone.

# CHAPTER FIVE

"The brave Garon was near death," Mountain said as Claus carried the bucket of water into the cabin. The giant was gently bandaging the wolf's wounds. Kama, the raccoon, watched.

"A mad bear—he is called Noluv—drove Garon's pack onto a mountain top. The snow-bridge they crossed collapsed." Mountain tied off a bandage.

"One of Garon's pack died in the fall and Noluv killed another. Sobaka and the survivors are trapped."

Claus nodded, "The bear, I know—it was he who drove me into these mountains. But who is Sobaka?"

Mountain finished his bandaging and stood. "Sobaka is the Wisest of Wolves."

Claus shrugged, "He must not be too wise, to get trapped on a mountain top."

Mountain stared down at the boy. "You are

young, Claus. Only two of Sobaka's pack died. Noluv would have killed them all." Claus was embarrassed but Mountain brushed it off quickly. "We must go. The ropes, Kama."

The raccoon scampered toward the door while Mountain moved around the cabin, gathering supplies.

Claus stood in silence until Mountain bellowed at him. "Go with him, quickly!"

Claus jumped for the door and hurried after Kama. The raccoon led the way to a snow-covered mound but when Kama began to scratch away at the hill, Claus understood and joined him.

Soon they uncovered a wooden door. The heavy door opened into a mountain-sized shed that held tools and ropes and…a sleigh big enough for a giant or four regular-sized adults. Claus admired the beautiful red sleigh until Kama hissed for him to grab the ropes and be quick about it.

Back in the cabin, Mountain was making Garon as comfortable as possible.

"Do not worry, my friend," the giant said quietly. "We will save your pack as you saved the boy." Mountain picked up his bag and a tiny halter covered with silver sleighbells and joined Kama outside.

"Where is the boy?" Mountain asked, as he put the belled halter on the raccoon. Kama squeaked a bit and ran several jingling steps toward the river. "Good," replied Mountain, "We will need the sled—the boy's legs are short."

Soon, Mountain's giant steps had carried them deep in the mountains; they had spoken little. Claus and Kama rode atop the coils of ropes which had been piled on Claus' sled. As they moved along a narrow path on the side of a mountain, Claus finally broke the silence.

"Mountain," asked Claus, "how did you find out about the wolves' danger?"

"Garon told me," answered the giant.

"You can talk with the animals?"

Mountain stopped and looked deep into the boy's eyes. "It is a great gift, talking with the animals. A gift you must earn."

Claus was silent and Mountain walked on.

Then the boy spoke again. "Mountain," Claus asked, "why is Kama wearing sleighbells?"

Mountain trudged on through the snow. "They are magic sleighbells, made by an ancient silver-smith, a dwarf named Randay."

Claus was very surprised, "How did you come by them?"

"A gift for a favor," replied Mountain.

"What was the favor?" continued Claus.

"I saved him from drowning. Dwarves are not, as a rule, strong swimmers.

"And what is their magic?" asked Claus.

Mountain sighed and stopped. He was tired of the questions. "The joyful sound. Did you not smile when you heard them?"

Claus nodded, remembering. Mountain began to walk again. "That is one of their powers."

Claus waited for more details, but the giant did not continue.

Finally, the boy asked, "What other magic rests in the bells, Mountain?"

Mountain stopped again, "You ask many questions, Young Claus. The bells give the wearer the strength of a hundred. Any more questions now?"

"Just one," answered Claus. "If the bells give the wearer the strength of a hundred, why do you not wear them now?" Claus smiled, feeling very cocky.

Mountain looked deeply into the boy's eyes. "Because Randay the Silversmith was no fool. The strength of a hundred humans in one is too frightening to think about. The sleighbells' magical strength is for our four-legged brothers and sisters only." Mountain nodded. "Randay was a wise dwarf."

With that, Mountain turned and continued the journey. Not wanting to disturb Mountain again, Claus began to think. His thoughts soon turned to Elder Anna and Baby Anna. He almost cried again as he thought of the lonely little girl back at the orphanage. He turned to Kama and spoke quietly to the curious raccoon.

"If I'd had the strength of a hundred men— boys—I could have saved Elder Anna." But, knowing that he did not, Claus soon began to feel sorry for himself again.

Then he brightened a bit. "Mountain...," he began.

The giant stopped but was obviously not listening to the boy. Young Claus fell silent and strained his ears. In the distance, they could hear the trapped wolves baying weakly and Noluv roaring mightily. The sled jerked forward as Mountain set off at a faster pace.

As they neared the sound of Noluv's roar and the wolves' howling, Claus wondered what they would do against so fierce a bear.

Then Mountain spoke the raccoon's name. Kama leaped off the sled and raced ahead, sleighbells jangling with every step. Claus watched the brave raccoon speed away, then looked up at Mountain, who spoke without slowing down.

"Now you'll see Randay's bells at work!"

Mountain and Claus burst into the clearing at the cliff's edge just in time to see Noluv roar and charge Kama, then stop, confused. Kama shook the sleighbells and charged the huge bear. Noluv roared, stumbled, fell, and scrambled away from the happy sound of the magic sleighbells. Claus was astonished. The tiny, jingling raccoon chased the ferocious, roaring bear far into the woods before turning around to join his friends.

When the pack saw the giant and the boy, the howls turned to barks of welcome as the wolves scrambled toward the edge of the sloping snow platform.

Suddenly, an unmistakable growl rose above the chaos at the mountain's edge. The wolves fell quiet and backed apart to make a path for Sobaka. The Wisest of Wolves' pride and dignity suffered no damage from his wounds or hunger. He limped, but made it seem like a badge of honor. At the cliff's edge, he stopped and howled a proud thank you across the chasm to the giant. Mountain was already unloading the sled. He paused.

"Thank me not yet, Wise Sobaka. You are still there."

Claus helped Mountain unload heavy ropes and wooden pulleys, a reindeer harness, and some shorter, thinner ropes.

"What will you do?" Claus asked.

"We must secure a rope to both sides. With the pulleys and this reindeer harness, we will pull the wolves across one by one."

Claus nodded as he helped lay out the harness. "This harness," Claus noted, "is much too large. What if the wolves struggle?"

Mountain spoke quietly. "They will fall. Each must summon his own courage to face the fear." By the time the rigging was ready, the wolves had grown restless. Sobaka was lying near the collapsed bridge. His growl silenced the pack again.

Claus was looking down across the gap that lay between the rescue party and the wolves. A frown was on his face—the sheer fall would certainly be fatal.

"Mountain," he asked, "how will you tie the rope to the other side? The wolves cannot tie a knot."

Mountain was talking quietly with Kama. Suddenly, the raccoon curled into a tight ball, then straightened out again.

Mountain stood up. "You are right, as usual, Kama. Round is best." Mountain finally turned his attention to the boy, "What did you ask?"

"Nimble fingers are required to tie knots, Mountain. How will you anchor the rope on the other side?"

Mountain smiled at the boy. "Clearly, lad, someone small must be thrown across the chasm."

Claus nodded and turned to glance a Kama; the frown returned. "But Kama's hands are too small."

Mountain nodded, "This is true."

Claus' frown grew deeper as he slowly turned to look up at the smiling giant. Then the boy's eyes widened.

Mountain spoke again, "You, Young Claus, are the wolves' only chance. Kama suggests you roll yourself into the shape of a river stone." He is right. Round is best.

Claus looked up at the giant: "A round stone?"

# CHAPTER SIX

Mountain picked the boy up to check his weight, then searched until he found a large stone of similar size. He lifted it to his shoulder then walked as close as he dared to the edge of the cliff. With a mighty roar, he heaved the boulder across the gap, sending the wolves howling away from the stone. The boulder thudded onto the other side, two yards beyond the great gap. But the round stone found no handhold on the icy slope and rolled quietly off the edge. The echo of the stone crashing down the mountain made Claus blink. There was a total silence from the wolves as they listened, too.

Sobaka slowly stepped forward and howled again to the giant. After a moment Mountain replied, "I understand Wise One."

In a few seconds, Mountain had tied the largest rope around Claus' waist The giant lifted the boy onto his shoulder, "You must become as round as the oldest riverstone and as light as the lightest feather."

Claus, aware that the time for fear was over, curled himself as tightly as possible before Mountain shifted his human rock onto his huge hand.

The wolves and Kama watched silently as Mountain took several gigantic running steps and hurled the boy across the deep abyss. The rope snaked out behind him as he flew over the ten thousand foot drop.

Claus hit the frozen slope with a thud and a yelp and immediately began to slide toward the edge of the snowbridge. Sobaka barked as he leaped forward, snapping his teeth into Claus' clothing so he could haul him back to safer ground. "Thank you Sobaka!" said Claus as he lay back and took a deep breath.

He was interrupted by Mountain, "Young Claus, the time to sleep is when the work is done."

Claus sighed and clambered to his feet, looking for an outcropping of rock that would anchor the rope. Soon, all was secure and they were ready for their first passenger. The wolves who had howled loudest for rescue now began to slink away in fear. No one wanted to be first this time. Sobaka snapped a command. Zago, one of the three wolves who wanted to eat Claus on the hillside, froze. Sobaka snarled again.

Claus carefully put the reindeer harness on the cowardly wolf and signaled to Mountain. The giant began to slowly pull the rope that was attached to the halter.

But as soon as the wolf's feet left the ground, he began to struggle. When he swung over the short, frozen slope that almost claimed Claus, his fear took over and he began to snap at the halter, lunging and growling until, finally, he fell.

Zago's death-howl echoed long after the cowardly wolf disappeared into the mountainside far below. Claus looked at Mountain, then at Sobaka. Sobaka stood, balanced himself, and walked with pride to stand beside Young Claus. The boy immediately helped Sobaka into the harness. Sobaka looked deep into Claus' eyes.

The bravest of wolves rode majestically across the great chasm perfectly still and controlled. In a matter of seconds, he was safe. The pack burst into howls of joy.

With Sobaka's example to guide them, the wolves calmly rode across the deep hole that had swallowed their brothers and sisters. A pair of cubs, far too small for the harness, made their ride in Claus' hat. The cubs, almost as still as their leader, Sobaka, were just as proud as he.

After the last wolf was safely on solid snow, Claus himself climbed into the halter and Mountain pulled him across to the yelps and barks that serve as cheers to wolves.

Sobaka stood tall and growled a solemn speech of thanks to the boy. Claus didn't understand the wolf's language, but he knew he was being thanked. Mountain, dressing the wounds of another wolf, looked up and translated only the last sentence.

"This pack and all its descendants will be friends to Claus forever."

The evening after they rescued the wolves,

Claus was deep in thought. After a cold night in the open, he, Kama, and Mountain had said good-bye to the wolf pack and started home. They were near Mountain's cabin now. Claus was silent, as he had been for most of the journey. He was tired, too, because he had walked (very quickly to keep up with the giant) most of the way. At times he also pulled the sled, and carried Kama, so Mountain would have a lesser burden. But now Claus was riding on the sled as the giant pulled it up to his home and stopped.

Mountain dropped his sled rope and stretched. Claus climbed off the sled and stood as tall as he could stand.

"Mountain…" Claus paused until his huge friend finished his stretch. "I must return to the orphanage now. Yesterday, I was needed by the wolves. Today, I am needed by the children."

Mountain frowned, "Young friend, again I say, follow your star. Do not reach for the stars of others."

Claus thought about the giant's words for a moment, then stiffened his resolve.

"Tomorrow, I leave," Claus said firmly.

Mountain smiled and nodded, "As I knew you would. Come, Young Claus, you must sleep."

# CHAPTER SEVEN

The next morning, Claus rose with the sun. Silently, Mountain helped him pack food and blankets on the sled. But as Claus prepared to tighten the ropes, the giant spoke.

"Hold a moment, young friend." Mountain disappeared into the cabin for a moment, then returned with a small, soft cloth bag. As he placed the bag on the top blanket, Claus heard the tiny, muffled jingle of sleighbells.

Mountain kneeled to look into the surprised boy's eyes.

"There are secrets," Mountain began, "Rules. The bells possess magic only for those who are giving enough to use them properly. Although humans may not grow stronger through Randay's bells, they control the animals who wear them. The bells must be given as a gift, given with respect and used with respect."

Mountain paused. "Young Claus, my respect

for you is shown by this gift. May Randay's bells serve you well."

Claus stood proudly, feeling as tall as the giant who kneeled before him. "I thank you, Mountain, and I will work hard to keep that respect."

Mountain, Kama, and Taku walked with Claus to the river. On its frozen surface, they stopped and Mountain unrolled a parchment map.

"Follow the river Delvin to where it becomes two rivers. The right branch, Delvin West, is your path home. But it divides into three. The left drops over Everfall and off all maps. The middle branch ends in the Lake of the Hollies. The right is, again, the path you take. It will guide you to your village."

The giant's eyes grew moist. He picked up the boy and gave him a gentle giant's hug.

Claus returned the embrace. "I will miss you, Mountain."

"And I will miss you, Claus."

Claus suddenly realized that, for the first time, the giant had not called him "young". When

Mountain put him down on the ice, the boy stood straight, nodded his head to the giant, then marched proudly away, pulling his precious sled and its valuable lessons and contents behind him.

Claus made good time down the frozen river. For most of the day, his journey was marked only by occasional small forest creatures who greeted him warmly.

"If only I could talk with the animals," thought Claus, "this trip would be more pleasant."

But Claus' thoughts were interrupted by a huge roar in the distance. He stopped to listen. Sure enough, a distant angry growl greeted his ears. The boy hurried in the direction of the noise, which grew louder with every turn in the river.

Soon, Claus figured out that Noluv lay ahead, apparently held at bay by someone or something.

The boy slid to a stop on the ice, untied his baggage, and drew out the sleighbell bag. He opened it and found a half-dozen of Randay's magic bells sewn onto a long cloth strap. Claus jerked the rope tight on his sled, threw the bells around his neck and over his shoulders like a jolly, jingling scarf, then headed on down river to face the ferocious Noluv.

By the sound of it, thought Claus, the raging bruin and his tormentor were just around the next bend. Claus sped up, his sled bouncing behind, the sleighbells jangling their happy sound. Claus rounded the bend at full speed, almost skating on the ice.

Dead ahead, he saw a tiny figure pop up from the rocks above the river and hurl a wooden spool at the furious bear. The spool caught Noluv solidly on his huge snout. The bear started to roar, then stopped. The sound of sleighbells had met his ears. Then he saw Claus and his rage overpowered his fear. With a stupendous roar, he charged the boy. Claus was shocked by the bear's response and tried to slow down on the slippery ice. But the bells finally did their work when the slow-witted bear heard them constantly between roars. Noluv slowed, stumbled, and went sprawling on the frozen river as he scrambled to escape the happy sound of

Claus' magic sleighbells.

Claus chased the bear into the snow-covered forest with a last shake of the sleighbell strap. Then he walked back to look at the scene of Noluv's latest fury. The river was littered with spools of thread and bolts of cloth.

Suddenly, a tiny figure, dressed in a flowing purple cape, leaped atop the rocks he had been hiding behind. He was joined quickly by another, whose more modest clothing was the color of the darkest evergreens. They both jumped to the ice. The little man in green carried a bag which he began to fill with the scattered dry goods. The caped figure walked with a swagger toward Claus.

They were no taller than the boy but both had long flowing beards and looked very old. The "green man" had white hair and a white beard; he was by far the oldest. The beard of the "caped man" was salt and peppery, but he was still very old. With a gasp, Claus realized that he had rescued two elves!

Claus met the caped elf halfway across the

river. The little man glanced this way and that as if to some audience besides the boy.

"I," the elf paused for effect, "am Gorkin, of White Mountain, artisan by tradition, thespian by nature. "This," he pointed to the other elf, "is my older brother, Belkin." Belkin looked up briefly, waved a friendly hand, then resumed gathering their things. Gorkin spoke again, "My brother is Keeper of the Animals."

The showy elf looked directly into Claus' eyes before he made his deepest actor's bow with a wide flourish of his cape. "With all the greatest and most profound and completely encompassing expressions of appreciative gratitude, summoned from the deepest recesses of our bottomless innermost beings, in the gravest and most solemn consideration of your heroic and aptly timed entry into our dramatic and dangerous battle with the evil bruin, whom we repelled with courage, imagination and well thrown spools of thread and bolts of cloth, and whom you frightened away despite the lack of fear-inducing qualities in your appearance... your appearance…" The elf had forgotten his next line. Panic filled his face.

From behind him, Belkin, his bag full now, whispered, "We thank you."

"Oh… we thank you, we thank you, we thank you again." With that, Gorkin bowed again, with the same flourish of his cape, then straightened, whirled on his heel and marched away before Claus could say a word.

The elf walked up to his brother as the boy watched. "You didn't have to tell me, I would have remembered."

Belkin smiled and handed his brother the bag, "Hearth and hospitality, brother, you forgot that, too." Belkin's voice was gentle, almost like music.

Gorkin blushed a deep red as his mind raced to compose a suitable speech to apologize and to offer the boy food and shelter.

Belkin moved to stand in front of Claus. "Your name, lad?" Claus was glad this elf was not as loud and flashy as the other.

"Claus, sir," he answered.

"Friend Claus," said the elf solemnly, "we are

elfin-bound to offer you hearth and hospitality for your act of kindness and bravery. Will you accept?"

All thoughts of Baby Anna and his pledge were swept aside by the thought of visiting with elves.

"Yes," Claus tried to be as solemn as Belkin and as dramatic as Gorkin, "I accept with great and gracious goodness."

Belkin smiled, nodded his head, then looked into the forest and whistled. A reindeer pulled a small sleigh from the woods just as Gorkin hurried up with another speech prepared.

"Friend Claus..." Gorkin began, bowing his head with embarrassment.

But Belkin interrupted him. "He has accepted, Gorkin."

Gorkin was obviously disappointed that he couldn't make his speech so Claus spoke up kindly. "If you would like, Friend Gorkin, you may ask me again anyway."

Belkin nodded, impressed with Claus' thoughtfulness, then shook his head, knowing what was in store for them.

Gorkin's face lit up and he grinned ear-to-ear, then struck a dramatic pose. "Friend Claus…"

But Belkin interrupted again. "At least, hold off until we have loaded the sleigh, little brother." Gorkin started to argue but when Claus immediately pitched in to help, he did the same.

In just a few moments, the sleigh was turned upright, the cloth and thread loaded, Claus' red sled tied to the back, and the boy and the two elves were being pulled down the river's bank by a reindeer with no reins.

Belkin whistled again, a different sound this time, and a hawk soared into view, then dived for the sleigh to land lightly on Belkin's shoulder. The Keeper of the Animals spoke quietly to the hawk, then the beautiful bird launched itself into the sky and flew quickly out of sight.

Gorkin struck his pose. The "actor elf" was still delivering his apology as they came to the great Delvin Divide. They followed Claus' path home until they reached the point where Delvin West split into three smaller rivers. The reindeer followed the left branch, toward Everfall. Soon, he turned off the river.

Gorkin was working on his invitation as the frozen river-road disappeared in the forest behind them. The reindeer, Vanguard, pulled the tiny sleigh, its three passengers, and Claus' red sled through a snow-bound forest on a path that seemed to open magically before them.

# CHAPTER EIGHT

Claus finally figured out (during one of Gorkin's many long, boring speeches) that the trail twisted and turned so often, you just couldn't see the open path ahead. There were also a great many other trails that criss-crossed the one they were on. Claus was amazed that Vanguard could follow the right path so easily. When Gorkin paused, Claus mentioned his thoughts to Belkin.

The old elf smiled, "the reindeer of White Mountain know their own trails. It is one of their greatest strengths."

Then Gorkin was off again, describing in great detail, how he had once played the role of Mullander, a famous elfin hero who led the world's greatest elves to White Mountain a thousand years before.

Claus settled back and began to think about how old the elves seemed. Nasha was the oldest person in his village; she was said to be a hundred and three. Claus' new friends looked to be four or five times that old, but were more lively than poor old Nasha. The boy decided to ask an elf about it sometime.

Suddenly, Vanguard pulled the sleigh into a clearing and stopped. The tiny frozen meadow rested at the foot of a huge white mountain. The mountain peak glistened in the evening sunlight above the forest. Gorkin took a deep breath and jumped from the sleigh to strike a dramatic pose in the center of the clearing.

"We have returned," he began dramatically, with a great flourish and bow.

Claus looked around but saw no audience, only frozen, gnarled trees.

"From the deepest depths of danger and despair, entered after completing our assignation of barter with the Linen Dwarves of Addon Delta, trapped on the river path by the most evil of all possible evil bruins, whom we held at bay with well-thrown spools and bolts of cloth, finally rescued by this brave young man of gentle features." Gorkin took another deep breath for what Claus thought would be another flood of fancy words. But with another flourish of his cape, Gorkin announced, "Claus!"

Claus was quite surprised when he heard his name end Gorkin's brief introduction. He almost thought he heard applause, then remembered that he was in the middle of a forest. Then he knew he heard it, faint, not from a large audience but a small one. He looked around the clearing for the sound. Slowly, very slowly, eyes and noses and hair and beards and hands and arms and legs and bodies were forming in the gnarled tree trunks that surrounded the snow-covered meadow.

The hands were clapping as a dozen ancient elves emerged from their hidden places in the trees. They were black and brown and white, men and women, dressed in different elfin costumes from their native lands. Claus' mouth fell open in surprise as he watched the little men and women move into the clearing. Their faces were friendly, but their smiles were not strong. Their polite applause tapered off and a wise and elderly woman stepped forward and, with a stately nod of her head, offered her hand and addressed the boy.

"You honor us by your presence, brave Claus. We thank you, we thank you, we thank you again for the rescue of our friends. Our mountain...," she indicated the huge snow-covered peak behind her, "is your mountain."

Claus bowed deeply, in the manner of Gorkin. "I thank you, I thank you, I thank you again."

"Yes... yes... well... yes. I am Gretanbar, Current High Mayor of White Mountain." She smiled at the boy, "Welcome to our home, Young Claus." Claus smiled back.

Then Gretenbar spoke quickly, "Come, come, now, we must move inside... the boy must be hungry and tired."

Gorkin and the other elves hustled when their High Mayor spoke. Claus moved quickly, too, but not before glancing over his shoulder to see about his sled. Two elves had picked it up and were following them. Belkin, Vanguard, and the sleigh had disappeared.

The elves led Claus into a magic opening in

the frozen mountain. In truth, it was only a maze through the ice, zigging and zagging, like the "invisible" path in the forest. Soon, the tunnel grew dark and they began to walk up a sloping floor. Claus knew they were in the mountain itself. He could barely see the elves, who moved swiftly even in the dark. Claus barely managed to keep up.

Suddenly, the elves stopped and Claus crashed into them. He apologized as Gretenbar shoved open a heavy wooden door. The dim light was blinding at first, but Claus' eyes adjusted quickly to the glow of firelight. They entered a long narrow cavern. There was no fire visible. The flickering reds and dancing yellows that filled the cavern were coming from holes in the towering rock walls. Dozens of warm windows and doors were chiseled into the stone at all levels. Rock paths and stairs led from door to door to floor. The huge cave was quiet except for their footsteps.

Gretenbar led the group across the cavern floor toward another tunnel.

"This is our first Corridor," announced Gorkin.

"In White Mountain, every citizen has a niche."

They entered the next cavern near the top and stood face-to-face with glistening crystal stalactites that hung from the ceiling. The firelight seemed to dance inside them—shimmering flecks of blue and green, with a bit of red. Then Claus looked down. The only sound after his gasp was the knickety-knack of tiny chisels and knives and sewing needles.

# CHAPTER NINE

From wall to wall, the cavern floor was filled with elves at workbenches, tools whickering in and out, in and out. Other elves pushed wooden carts loaded with carving wood and cloth and finished crafts in and out of the tunnels that surrounded the giant elfin workshop. Claus stood and stared, trying to take it all in.

There were black elves and brown elves and white elves and yellow elves. There were toy elephants and horses and dolls and wagons and tops and funny pop-up jesters. Sheep with wheels and geese without. Reed-carved flutes and paper-head drums. But, still, the only sound was the knickety-knack, knickety-knack of tiny elfin tools.

"Our workshop" said Gretenbar, proudly. "We are toymakers." Then Gretenbar urged the group down the stone steps to the floor of the workshop. The other elves paid little attention to Claus and his party as Gretenbar led them through the workshop toward another tunnel. Claus stared in silence as the toymakers whittled and snipped and sewed and stacked.

Claus' amazement finally gave way to curiosity. "Tell me, High Mayor, what do you DO with the toys?" The boy had seen no children in White Mountain.

"Do?" asked Gretenbar, "do?" She was puzzled by the question. "Why, we store them of course. For The Purpose." She shook her head at what she thought was a rather silly question.

"But," Claus persisted, "what IS the Purpose?"

"Hmph, harumph. Yes . . . well . . . well . . . ," Gretenbar's voice turned sad. "THAT we do not know. We trade our crafts with the Linen Dwarves for the cloth and thread to make more toys. But we do not know why we make them."

They neared a tunnel and Claus threw a last glance at the wonderful workshop.

"Come along, now, Young Claus," said Gretenbar, "table is ready."

The tunnel from the workshop opened into a

cave that was even larger than the one they left. "The Great Hall," announced Gorkin, "here we meet and here we eat." The Great Hall held row after row of neat tables and chairs.

Claus' eyes lit up when the aroma of fresh bread greeted his nose. Odd cooking smells— different from those at the orphanage—mixed with the bread-smell to set Claus' nose all a'tingle. As his group headed for the front table, two elves in aprons emerged from another tunnel, carrying trays of steaming dishes and baskets of nuts and bread.

The High Mayor pulled a chair from the table and offered it to Claus. The chair fit well, the food smelled great, and Claus was starved. His escorts moved around the table to sit down. Claus noticed that dinner was eaten in silence. Claus was very anxious to ask questions about the toys, but he knew it would be rude to break the elves' tradition of silent meals. Claus wondered how the Mother Superior at the orphanage would react to silence at the table; he decided she would probably faint.

When Claus finished his meal, Gretenbar turned to him. "Claus, your niche in White Mountain has been prepared."

Claus liked that idea, if it meant bed. He was tired to the bone. The High Mayor led Claus to yet another sleeping corridor and his own private niche.

As the hearty meal settled in his stomach, Claus settled into a soft, goose-down mattress and quickly fell asleep. All night, he dreamed of caverns full of toys of every description, each calling out to be played with.

Claus woke up slowly. When he could focus his eyes, he sat up and looked around his niche. An elfin/boy-sized table, bookshelf, stuffed chair, and the goose-down bed were the only furnishings. A friendly fire greeted him from the fireplace and gave the tiny cave a cheery glow. His sled was in the corner, still loaded with his things.

Claus took his time standing up. He arched his back and stretched his arms up and almost broke his fingers on the low stone ceiling. The boy rubbed his hands and fingers to ease the pain as he walked over to look out his doorway. Claus realized that he was very hungry again and quickly made his way to the Great Kitchen.

Almost as soon as Claus finished his silent breakfast, alone in the Great Hall, Gorkin appeared to guide him on a tour of White Mountain. Claus was ready—he knew he would be seeing those toy caverns he had dreamed of all night. Gorkin was in fine spirits too; here was an excellent opportunity to practice his oratorical projections.

They barely made it through Gorkin's first speech and the first toy-room before Claus broke away and dived into the pile of toys that filled the huge cavern, kicking and waving, laughing and shouting at the top of his young voice.

Gorkin's solemn face suddenly wrinkled—he smiled, then grinned, then burst into happy laughter at the sight of the boy's unbridled joy. Gorkin's laughter begin to build and bounce and echo through the great network of caves and corridors, niches and caverns. Soon every elf in

White Mountain was laughing, though only those closest to Toy Room Ten knew why.

The day Young Claus dived into those toys and made Gorkin laugh was the first time the elves had laughed in hundreds of years! They really didn't CARE why they were laughing - it felt good and sounded good, so they all joined in until every niche and cave echoed with the sound of happy elves. The very mountain itself seemed to chuckle and the animals throughout the forest looked up and smiled.

Eventually, when Claus fell exhausted on the pile of toys, the laughter began to die down and other voices took its place.

First, the reason for the joy was spread from elf to elf, "The boy's in the toys!… The boy's in the toys!… The boy's in the toys!…" On and on, the word spread. Until someone, in some niche, in some small corner of the great mountain, reversed the flow of the nodding and proclaimed gravely, "The Purpose."

Then the caverns were filled with the solemn pronouncement, "The boy is the purpose…

Claus is the Purpose…the boy is the Purpose…
Claus is the Purpose!"

Claus and Gorkin heard none of the talk. The
boy was playing with the toys more calmly, first
one, and then another, and then another while
Gorkin watched him, smiling.

Far away in the network of caves, High Mayor
Gretenbar was meeting with an elf dressed in a
flowing hooded robe the color of healthy earth.
Flecks of silver and gold and red sparkled in the
strange elf's brown robe.

Gretenbar spoke respectfully to the hooded
elf. "So, Wizard, you believe the boy Claus is,
indeed, the Purpose we have waited centuries to
find?"

The voice of the hooded elf was vaguely familiar. "A portion, High Mayor, a portion. I would
speak to him at length to discover more."

"Yes," said Gretenbar, "that is wise. And try to
find out how such a youth could frighten the
likes of Noluv."

# CHAPTER TEN

Claus was still in Toy Room Ten. Gorkin had not really noticed, but Claus was growing bored. Something was missing. Claus rolled a wagon across the smooth cavern floor to... no one. And no one, of course, rolled it back. Gorkin didn't even think of it because elves only make toys, they don't play with them. As Claus sighed, another elf entered the room to speak quietly to the actor elf.

Claus followed the elf Kristoval through a series of tunnels until they entered a large cave. High on one wall, Claus could see a niche. That was their destination.

"The Wizard's niche," announced Kristoval. This niche was far larger than Claus'. But the greatest difference was the way it was furnished.

The niche was filled with the things you would expect to see in a wizard's cave. Cubbyholes and shelves cut into the stone held tiny boxes and bags of who-knows-what. Clear bottles of all sizes and shapes held colorful liquids, fine powders, and herbs and roots of all descriptions. Wooden shelves and tables held books and bottles and all manner of odd tools, measuring devices, and strange mechanical contraptions.

Toys of all kinds littered the room—odd and new, experimental and proven. Claus' eyes blinked as he tried to take it all in. He saw a hawk sitting calmly on its perch, eating seeds from a small bowl. He recognized the bird as the one who had landed on Belkin's shoulder at the river. They moved deeper into the cave until Claus saw the hooded elf sitting at a workbench.

The hooded elf turned to face them. It was Belkin!

Claus' mouth dropped open in surprise. The Keeper of the Animals, the Wizard of the Mountain—they were the same person. Claus had thought Belkin was something like a stable boy, only very old.

"Thank you, Kristoval." With a nod, Kristoval

left the boy with the elfin wizard.

"I am sorry," Belkin began, "that we did not have the opportunity to talk on our journey to White Mountain. My younger brother tends to forget about others when he is speaking. It is his greatest weakness. You must have many questions by now, Young Claus. I would like to try to answer them and then ask you a few."

Claus had recovered from realizing that the elf he believed to be a stable hand was really a respected wizard. "How old are you?" he asked.

Belkin took a deep breath, "To tell you the truth, I don't remember. Something over eight hundred twenty seven in your years, as far as I can recall... or maybe it was six hundred twenty seven."

Claus asked the next question very slowly, "Will you live forever?" Belkin grew a bit uncomfortable and took a moment to reply. "I'm afraid I can't answer that question."

Claus was surprised. "Why not?"

Belkin squirmed in his seat a bit, "Because... because I don't know."

"You mean you don't know if you're going to die or not?" asked Claus.

"Well," Belkin answered, "to my knowledge, an elf has never died. We believe it has something to do with White Mountain. Since Mullandar led us here almost a thousand years ago, no one has died."

Belkin changed the subject while Claus was still thinking about living forever.

"My turn. Mine is a question I have wanted to ask since we met on the frozen Delvin—how did you frighten the evil Noluv so easily?"

Claus shrugged, "The sleighbells."

"But where did you get sleighbells with such magic?' asked Belkin.

Claus told him, "A giant, named Mountain, gave them to me."

Belkin looked at Claus like he didn't believe him.

"But I have always heard that giants ate little boys... and elves."

"Not this giant," said Claus. "He's the only one I know and he didn't eat me." Claus grinned, "Of course, I'm not sure about elves, but I don't believe he would eat them either."

Belkin chuckled. "But how do the bells work?" Claus told the elfin wizard all he knew about the magic silver sleighbells. Belkin was surprised at the bells' magic strength but he was not at all surprised that it only worked for animals.

"Would you like to see them?" Claus asked Belkin.

"Oh yes, very much," the Wizard answered.

Claus ran to his niche, then quickly returned with the sleighbell bag. Belkin examined the bells carefully after putting a tiny pair of wire-frame eyeglasses on his nose.

After a moment, the wizard looked up. "If you are agreeable, Young Claus, I would like to experiment with the bells."

Claus didn't understand what an "experiment" was but when Belkin explained it was a test of the magic, he agreed.

The wizard was carrying a reindeer harness with one silver sleighbell attached and was leading Claus through another small tunnel that led from the niche into the next cavern. This room was the Cave of Animals. The animals' cavern was smaller than the Great Hall but larger than the sleeping corridors. There were no stalls, just food and water troughs carved into the stone.

Reindeer were eating and drinking and just standing around. Dozens of other animals also made this cave their home—rabbits, squirrels, fox, a wolf or two, an otter, several raccoons and an ancient moose who seemed on the verge of dying.

Except for the troughs, the cave was natural, with nooks and crannies and smaller crevices between its stone walls. Looking more closely, Claus saw a niche up on the wall, but it was dark; no warm fire lit the window and door.

The boy and the elfin wizard threaded their way through the herd of deer toward the moose. Belkin patted the reindeer and called them by name. The floor was covered with wild hay that glistened bright yellow in the sunlight.

Suddenly, Claus stopped. Sunlight? "But we're inside a mountain," he thought. He looked up to see hundreds of small round holes hidden among the crystal stalactites. By moving around, Claus could see that each hole was a long, straight tunnel that led to the outside of White Mountain to bring in daylight.

Belkin noticed the boy's puzzlement. "The animals cannot fight fire."

"But, Wizard Belkin," asked Claus, "How do you keep the light shafts open? Is it magic?" Belkin, surprised, stopped to look up and move his head around, studying the long shafts of light. He chuckled, "It certainly looks like it, doesn't it?" Then he walked on, a smile on his face, the sleighbells jingling on the halter.

The ancient moose greeted Belkin with a weak snort. "Ah, Malek." Belkin put his arms around the moose's huge chest. "How are you feeling?"

Malek snuffled. Belkin's smile vanished and he sadly patted the moose's side. "Yes, Friend Malek, I know. Very soon. It saddens me."

Malek snuffled again and the wizard brightened. "Yes, yes, of course, you old moose, I know the time is always proper." Then Belkin turned to

Claus. "Friend Claus, " Belkin nodded, "This is Friend Malek, Retired Master of All White Mountain Moose Clans."

Malek snuffled and Claus smiled. "I am greatly honored, Master Malek."

The moose snuffled and shook his massive head and antlers. Belkin was puzzled.

"Friend Malek is not impressed with your respectful words. He says you have met before."

Suddenly, Claus remembered the moose he had frightened on the day he was separated from the other orphans. He looked at his feet in shame as he recognized the dying moose. Claus felt confused and followed Belkin sadly as the wizard left Sire Malek. The wise wizard asked no questions.

Vanguard, the reindeer, now followed them. He had joined the boy and the wizard when they stopped to talk to Malek. In a corner near the tunnel, Belkin hitched Vanguard to the tiny sleigh with the belled harness. Vanguard shook the bell with delight as he pulled the two "scientists" through a wide, twisting tunnel out onto a huge snowbound plateau high up on the side of White Mountain. The jingling sleighbells made Belkin and Claus chuckle. Vanguard stopped just outside the tunnel while Belkin told him the secret of the sunlit cave of the animals. He indicated dozens of pointed crystal rocks sticking up through the snow.

"We call those forms 'stalagmites'—they grow from the floor to meet the roof-dripper, which we call stalactites. Long ago, we fashioned holes in the roof of the cave, then moved the stalagmites from the bottom of the cavern to the outside of the mountain and set them over the holes. The animals have light with no fire."

Claus was impressed. Then they settled into their seats and gripped the sleigh.

"Please, Friend Vanguard," said Belkin, but Claus interrupted him.

"I almost forgot, Belkin," cried Claus. "I give the bell to you."

"Given? What is 'given'?" The wizard had never before received a gift.

"It is yours, to keep forever, or to give to someone else," explained Claus.

Belkin smiled and repeated the word, "given." The wizard was very pleased to receive his first gift. "Given." He turned to Vanguard. "Please, Friend, run!"

In a flash, the deer was off and streaking across the snow-covered mountain meadow. Fortunately, Vanguard had the sense to stop before they crashed into a snow bank or sailed off the mountain. Belkin and Claus were breathless!

"It's like he could fly," Claus whispered finally.

"And just one bell, Young Claus, just one bell," whispered Belkin. Then the wizard turned to the reindeer, "Vanguard, you were magnificent."

A few hours after the experiment with Vanguard, Claus moved into the niche in the Cave of Animals. This caused quite a stir among the elves—that niche had remained empty for two hundred years, ever since Belkin finished his apprenticeship and took Jezebeth's role as wizard. Was Claus the new apprentice? It was always an elf before. Was Claus really here to fulfill The Purpose? The workshop was no longer the silent factory. The cavern buzzed with talk and chuckles and growing interest. The boy noticed the change but did not know he was the cause.

# CHAPTER ELEVEN

For several days, Claus helped Belkin care for the animals and conduct further experiments with sleighbells. They discovered, for instance, that the bell helped Vanguard leap ten times as far as he could without them. Claus began to spend less time at play and more time at work. The animals liked the boy and he liked them. He also enjoyed the hours that he and Belkin spent improving the toys.

One day, they added color to the cloth; the next day, paint to the wood, brightening the toys to a gleam. When they presented their new models to a general session of the Grand Council, there was great applause and laughter, the first such outburst in the long history of White Mountain Grand Councils. From that day forward, a good number of toys were set aside for dyeing and for painting.

A few days after Claus and Belkin added color

to the toys, the wizard woke the boy gently. "Malek is leaving us, Claus. Come please."

The Cave of the Animals was empty. The animals of White Mountain were gathered outside on the meadow. Belkin finally spoke again as he and Claus walked toward the circle.

"Malek wanted you to witness his Ceremony of Separation. It is a great honor, Claus."

The boy, no longer confused, was overwhelmed by a feeling of great sadness. The animals stepped aside as Belkin moved into the ring they had formed around Malek. Claus slowly walked up to the great, tired, moose and stood with several elves. Malek lay on a bed of straw. His breathing was heavy and he coughed a bit. The old moose could not lift his head. Tears welled up in Claus until they finally crept into his eyes.

After a moment of silence, Belkin lifted his arms to the dawn sky. One star shined brightly; the others were dim because of the approaching daylight.

The Keeper of the Animals spoke slowly, with

great feeling. "Creator and Keeper of humans and beasts, God of all that is or ever will be, as Keeper of White Mountain's animals, I ask you to accept the gracious spirit of Sire Malek, Master of All White Mountain Moose Clans and ancient friend of your humble servant. May you guide Sire Malek to his final resting place beside your always peaceful waters. I pray you grant Sire Malek fields of everlasting clover."

Then Belkin bowed his head and closed his eyes. The animals did the same and Claus followed suit, saying a silent prayer for the dying moose and another for his own forgiveness.

Suddenly, the boy looked up and ran to the moose. "Sire Malek, forgive me."

Malek, after a moment, quietly snuffled and slowly placed his hoof in Claus' hand. Claus knew he had been forgiven.

A moment later, Belkin mumbled and he and the animals looked up. Claus felt the movement and opened his eyes. Malek was dead. Claus felt very sad and empty. Belkin put his arm around the boy's shoulders and led him back into the cave. The animals said their silent prayers, then slowly headed back to the cavern. The other elves stayed behind. When the plateau was empty, they buried Malek's body.

Later that day, Claus sat sadly in a toy room. He rolled a painted wagon across the floor to... no one. And no one, of course, rolled it back.

Malek's Ceremony of Separation brought back Claus' memories of the two Annas. So he just sat and looked at the toys; he didn't feel like playing with them. But then he picked up one of the funny pop-up jesters and thought how Baby Anna would love it, and realized that he would love to give it to her. Suddenly, his thoughts were interrupted by Belkin.

"Friend Claus, many of the elves in White Mountain believe you are The Purpose for which we have waited so long. Tonight, we shall discuss it in Grand Council."

The boy was quite surprised, but recovered quickly. "And you, Keeper," he asked, "What do you believe?"

Belkin replied slowly. "I believe you are in

some way here to serve the Purpose, but I believe nothing beyond that."

Belkin gave Claus a moment to think about his words, then spoke again. "Tonight, we hold a special session of The Grand Council to consider the issue. You are welcome to attend."

That night, the Great Hall was full. With all respect to High Mayor Gretenbar, she was not accustomed to dealing with such rowdy crowds. The laughter Claus brought to White Mountain had unleashed long buried emotions in the once-solemn elves. There was shouting, and laughter, and the stamping of feet as the magical elves argued the case of "Claus as Purpose."

"Why else would he be here?" asked one.

"But Belkin says he is not all," said another.

"His laughter brought us life… that must surely be a sign."

On and on they went, creating reasons after reasons for both sides. Claus was mystified by the event.

Finally, the High Mayor banged her staff loudly enough and long enough on the rock floor to get the attention of the Council.

When all was quiet, she spoke. "It has been proposed that we, the ruling Grand Council, give to Claus all of the toys we have stored for so many centuries."

Claus eyes widened and his mouth dropped open. The elves were puzzled until the High Mayor explained the word "Giving."

"Now, we shall vote," Gretenbar continued, "aye or nay. Are the counters in place?"

From around the Great Hall, a dozen elves perched on rock ledges called out their readiness.

"Then let the vote begin. All those who vote 'Aye,' raise your hands."

One by one, little hands spouted into the air until it was immediately clear that the 'Ayes' had it. All of the toys in White Mountain now belonged to Claus!

A great cheer and clamor arose as the elves began to celebrate. Claus was in ecstasy. All of the White Mountain toys were his—more toys than a child could ever even dream of. "Mine," thought Claus, "all mine." Wizard Belkin watched him thoughtfully.

That night, Claus could hardly sleep. First thing next morning he would count his toys. No, that would take too long—he would count the toy rooms instead. He would put the wooden birds in one cave and the wagons in another and the musical instruments in still another and... Claus finally drifted off to a restless sleep full of parties and flutes and dolls and animals and pop-up jesters.

Claus spent the entire next day playing with his toys. He did no work, fed no animals, improved no toys. He just played. Near the end of the day, after he had counted the thirty-two caves of toys a dozen times, he sat down in Toy Room Twelve with a strange look on his face, an odder feeling in his heart. He knew something was missing, but he could not remember what it was.

The next day, Claus was rousted out of bed by a grizzled elf named Jonathan who led the boy to breakfast, then to a decorating party in the first Corridor. The elves were still jolly from the night before and the idea of a celebration delighted them even further as they marched outside.

But Claus was not so happy. The emptiness he felt the day before still nagged him. Something was missing, but what was it?

Outside, the work party began to tie candles in the gnarled evergreens, that surrounded the clearing. Bright ribbons and crystal baubles on fine dwarf-made string, and tiny toys (replicas of the larger ones) were all hung carefully on the trees. Claus' unhappy mood began to lift a bit when he saw the glittering ornaments.

Claus was all the way across the meadow from the cave when he heard noises in the forest. He looked closely. Suddenly, his eyes widened in fear. Two ferocious-looking bears were racing straight at him.

Claus dropped his candles and decorations and raced for the cave shouting, "Bears, bears!"

The elves whirled to see Claus go down under two fuzzy bundles of brown fur, and then bounce and try to scramble away.

But the bears wouldn't stop. To their delight the elves, who clapped their hands and laughed, finally joined the free-for-all. You see, the bears were just cubs and only wanted to play. When Claus caught on, he roared with laughter from the bottom of the pile. Elves, boy, and "silly" bear cubs wrestled in the snow for a long time, going at it hands and paws.

Finally, the sound of Belkin clearing his throat broke through the noise of the wrestlers. They slowly pulled apart and the elves drifted back to their work, chuckling over the fun.

Claus stayed to watch Belkin kneel and whisper to the little bears. After a moment's conversation, the wizard stood and marched for the cave. The cubs followed and Claus caught up.

"Noluv attacked their winter den and killed their mother." Belkin spoke as he walked. "It is time to deal with the evil bruin. Tonight, the celebration will draw him to White Mountain. We must be ready."

After making the cubs comfortable in the Cave of the Animals, Claus joined Belkin in his niche. The wizard was studying an ancient map. Belkin touched the map with respect.

"The reindeer trails of Forest Yule. Vanguard's great-great-grandfather left it to Jezebeth. It is through these paths we must push Noluv."

"Push him where?" asked Claus.

Belkin sadly pointed to the end of a river that disappeared off the map. "Everfall!"

As night fell on White Mountain, the elves lit the candles in the trees around the meadow. It was almost magical, the way the candlelight sparkled off the crystal baubles. The Toymakers and the animals from the mountain were in joyous spirits. There was food to eat, drinks to drink, games to play, and a hundred songs to be sung. Soon the noisy crowd was joined by every forest creature in the area who wasn't asleep for the winter—and a few that had been.

Elves had dusted off flutes and mandolins and dulcimers and harps. The lovely music they played was as ancient as their instruments. Soon dancing began in both large and small circles, inside and out. Laughter was constant and rejoicing was the order of the night. The elves, in the glory of the hour, remembered old talents and arts—there were jugglers, acrobats, fire-eaters, and even elfin swamies! Gorkin and a few others were performing bits of Mullandar's story to loud applause and cheers.

At the edge of the meadow, Claus, Belkin, the bear cubs, and several brave elves were keeping an eye out and an ear open for the evil Noluv.

Suddenly, Belkin's hawk friend dropped from the sky to land on the wizard's shoulder. The Keeper of the Animals spoke to the hawk, then listened. Soon they heard Noluv bellowing far in the distance. The other elves and animals were so busy with their fun that they heard nothing but their own noises.

Belkin and the other ambushers joined forces to wait near the path Noluv seemed to be following. Closer and closer he came through the dark, cold forest. Now he was quieter, not wanting to alert his prey. Suddenly, Belkin was alone. He moved back, still facing the tunnel-like path. The wizard held a soft cloth bag out in front of him.

A split second later, the horrible bear roared into the clearing. The other elves and animals heard the noise and scattered to get away.

Belkin moved quickly—he jerked a sleighbell from the cloth bag and began to shake it with all his might. Noluv turned to stare, then shook his head and pawed his ears.

Slowly, Belkin moved toward the furious bear, who charged and retreated again and again. Noluv broke for a path to escape, but Claus barred his way with another bell. A cub, with a sleighbell tied around its neck, blocked the entrance to another trail. Finally, Belkin, cub, and Claus forced the bear to enter the path they had chosen. The others followed, whispering "Everfall," "Everfall," "Everfall."

On and on, they pressed, Noluv occasionally charging a few steps, only to turn around and try to escape again. At the first reindeer crossing, Noluv turned, only to face the hawk, a silver sleighbell tied to its leg, blocking the path. Now every trail was blocked by the elves, cubs, the hawk—every trail except the one leading to the steep, frozen cliffs of Everfall.

Noluv was beside himself with fear and

rage—and roared and charged, he backed away and began to pace the edge of the frozen falls, terrified for his life. Belkin stepped forward.

"Bruin Noluv, you are guilty of rampage throughout the Northern Range. Have you anything to say?" Noluv growled and bared his teeth. "Will you swear from this day forward to live in peace with all creatures?" Again, Noluv growled angrily.

Belkin's next words were spoken quietly. "Then we have no choice. Everfall must claim your soul."

The Keeper of the Animals slowly, sadly began to shake the sleighbells in his hands. Noluv roared, charged, then edged closer to his death.

Suddenly, Claus spoke. "Ask him why, Belkin, ask him why."

Belkin lowered his bells, wondering why he hadn't thought of that. The wizard looked directly into Noluv's evil eyes. "You heard the question, greatest of bears, why do you refuse to live in peace?"

The bear stopped pacing and growled, but not angrily. Belkin translated again, "Because all fear me."

Noluv growled again. Belkin was quite surprised at the bear's words. "To live in peace, one
must have something to love, someone to love,
someone who does not fear."

There was a deep silence at the edge of Everfall
that night.

Then, suddenly, Claus dropped his sleighbells
on the ice, and walked straight toward the confused bear.

Noluv roared and charged, then stopped when
Claus did not falter. The huge bear who had
brought so much fear and pain to the Northern
Range stood frozen in his place as the boy
named Claus stepped bravely up to put his hand
on Noluv's massive chest in a sign of friendship.
Noluv shivered, blinked, then embraced Claus in
the warmest bear-hug ever known to mankind.

Gretenbar and Gorkin led the cheers and
applause and shouts of joy and the winter star
that seemed to follow Young Claus shined brightly above all the rest.

When the company returned to the meadow,
the celebration began anew, this time with Noluv

the center of attention. Claus and Belkin watched him and smiled at each other as the huge bear danced with everyone.

Suddenly, Claus, his eyes bright and determined, turned to the wizard. "Tomorrow, Keeper, I leave White Mountain." Claus understood why he had felt so empty that day in toy room, because something was missing. It was his pledge.

# CHAPTER TWELVE

Early the next morning, Claus awoke to find his sled loaded with nuts and fruit and hard elfin candy. A bag of toys was tied beneath the food. Belkin entered Claus' niche; the boy was still stretching his sleep away.

The wizard handed Claus a map. "You should be home soon after nightfall. The animals will watch you along the way."

Two elves came in and picked up Claus' sled and carried it through The Cave of Animals. The reindeer and rabbits and raccoons and foxes and wolves... and Noluv... all came to nuzzle Claus a fond good-bye as he and Belkin crossed the cavern to join an escort led by Gretenbar, as usual, and followed by Gorkin. But by this time, the actor elf was almost silent.

As the boy walked through the workshop, the now lively elves gave him a cheer with a few shouts of "Remember The Purpose, Claus," and

"Come back soon, Claus," and "Your niche is always open, Claus."

Young Claus fought back his tears to smile and wave at his elfin friends. On the meadow, the sled-carrying elves put it down and said good-bye. Gretenbar and Gorkin wished Claus a long life, then left the boy and the wizard alone.

Claus said, "I will miss you, Wizard Belkin, Keeper of the Animals of White Mountain."

Belkin smiled, as if he knew something. "Now you must go or spend the night in the forest. I thank you for your gift of the sleighbells and hope the few you have kept will protect you on your journey." Claus' eyes were filled with tears.

Suddenly, Claus leaped forward to hug his elfin friend. Belkin returned the embrace warmly, shiny tears glistened in his ancient eyes. After a moment, the elf gently pushed Claus away.

"It is time." Claus picked up the rope to his sled and Belkin walked with him to the edge of the clearing just as daylight flooded the meadow.

The wizard put his hand on the boy's shoulder. "Good journey, Friend Claus."

With that, Belkin turned and walked back toward the cave entrance before Claus could say a word.

Suddenly, the wizard's hawk zoomed into the meadow and landed on the little elf's shoulder. With one long, last look at his beloved friend, Claus pulled his sled into the path.

---

It was just as Belkin had said—Claus' trip was pleasant, with animals of all kind sharing a few steps along the way. The sunlight disappeared only an hour or so before Claus topped the long hill that overlooked the village and the orphanage. Bright starlight and a glowing moon lit the scene below him. It was only then that he noticed a reindeer pacing him in the woods. Claus chuckled and waved.

"I have made it, friend deer. I thank you for your watchful eyes." Claus pointed to the dark orphanage and addressed the animal again. "There lies my future, friend deer, to make children laugh and help them live happy lives."

With that, Claus laughed and raced away from

the deer to jump on his sled and slide the rest of the way to the orphanage gate.

Quietly, carefully, Claus opened the gate and pulled his sled into the courtyard. The huge stone building was gray in the moonlight, casting strange dark shadows on the snow. Knowing exactly where he was going, Claus moved to the oldest part of the orphanage. He untied his bundles and placed the food bag inside of the toy bag, and threw the whole buddle over his shoulder. Then he climbed up to the roof of the tumbled-down wing of the building.

Then, quick as a flash, he slipped down an old chimney. It was clear that the long-cold fireplace was a familiar route.

The orphanage was quiet and dark when Claus crawled into the part of the building still being used. He made his way directly to the chapel and prayed a thank-you, then he blew out the candle that was still burning for him. Claus looked at the altar as he turned to leave, but stopped because he saw something he hadn't seen before. A tiny manger was displayed near the alter—and there, in the center of the nativity scene, was a small figure of a baby. It was Christmas Eve. The boy said another silent prayer of thanks.

From the chapel, Claus crept quietly into the long hall where the orphans dozed dreamily in two long rows of beds. Slowly, moving silently from bed to bed, Claus slipped a toy and some treats into the stockings that were hung to dry at the foot of each bed. A child would stir and Claus would drop out of sight, hiding behind the footboard. No one ever saw him.

At Baby Anna's side, Claus smiled when he saw her face and gave her two handfuls of treats and the prettiest doll.

Claus skipped only one bed—his own. He had thought it out and realized that Elder Anna may already have been replaced. After all, he had been gone almost two whole weeks. So he decided to take his old place if another leader slept in Elder Anna's bed. Taking a deep breath, Claus walked slowly toward the alcove where Elder Anna slept. His head bowed, he prayed that he would be worthy. At the bedside, he stopped, opened his eyes, and saw, with great disappointment, that Elder Anna's place had been filled. Then he looked closer to see who now slept in Elder Anna's alcove.

It was Elder Anna. Claus gasped with joy— Elder Anna rolled over, but Claus was too stunned to move. She did not awaken so Claus leaned over and gently kissed her cheek. Then he filled her stocking with treats and baubles and a silver sleighbell and happily made his way back to his bed. He quietly placed his bag down; it was empty but Claus' heart was full. He reached over to turn his blanket down and stopped cold. A sad little boy of four was sleeping restlessly in Claus' old bed.

At first, Claus was confused. He glanced up at Elder Anna's alcove, then back at the sleeping child. Suddenly, he felt very lonely. The orphanage no longer had a place for him. He smiled and tucked the little boy in, then reached for his bag and a toy. All he came up with was a small handful of kernels.

Then he thought of something.

First, he gathered back some of Elder Anna's treats—he knew she wouldn't mind—then raced outside, through the door this time.

In a moment, he returned, carrying his sled. His prized sled, his most cherished possession. When Claus placed that sled at the foot of the new boy's bed, that brightest star in the sky shined even more brightly through a window. A small tear glistened on Claus' cheek. Claus walked toward the sleeping hall door with a twinkle in his eye and a bounce in his step. As he opened the door, he turned for a last look at the children he loved.

At the foot of each bed, there was a tiny, gentle light shining from each stocking. Claus decided it was a beautiful sight. It reminded him of the night before, at White Mountain, the Celebration of Lights, as it came to be called. It was a happy moment for Claus.

Outside, he said good-bye to the old stone orphanage. It looked more silver than gray now. The boy moved quietly through the gate and looked up into the bright, starlit night. That brilliant star in the east, as always, shone brightest. Claus looked at it and smiled, and then started walking up the snow covered hill toward it.

Then he heard a lovely, familiar sound. The reindeer who had been pacing alongside him earlier was jingling up to his side.

"Greetings, again, Friend Deer. I am Claus, and you wear the bells of White Mountain."

The deer snuffled.

"Donner, I am pleased to meet you…"

Claus froze in his tracks. He could understand the deer's language. He understood! Claus could talk with the animals. He laughed and jumped and whooped and Donner joined him in the reindeer fashion, sleighbells jiggling and jangling.

Donner snuffled again. Claus beamed, "I would be honored."

The boy climbed onto the reindeer's back and Donner turned to 'kiss' him on the nose. Claus giggled and reached a finger up to rub his wet nose and, in a flash of brilliant light, the boy and the deer disappeared.

Claus' laughter rang out in the crisp winter night. It was quickly joined, on that cold

Christmas Eve, by the mighty guffaw of Mountain and the joyous chuckles of the Elves and finally, by the growing laughter of all the children of the world.

# THE END

SPECIAL THANK-YOUS ARE DUE TO:

*Jack Peterson, who, on a cold, clear mid-winter's eve long ago, said, "Have you ever thought about Santa as a little boy?"*

*All the editors at Cygnet Trumpeter who did such a great job, even lowering my reading time.*

*And, last of all, most of all, Tim Leary Swan, who not only believed in 'Claus', but did something about it, and made one of my fondest dreams come true.*